j
PB
Joseph

All Dressed Up and Nowhere To Go

Daniel M. Joseph and Lydia J. Mendel

Illustrated by Normand Chartier

Houghton Mifflin Company

Boston 1993

With special thanks
to Lydia's parents
and to Robin
—D.J. and L.M.

For Matthew and Sally Rubia—N.C.

Library of Congress Cataloging-in-Publication Data

Joseph, Daniel M.
  All dressed up and nowhere to go / Daniel M. Joseph and Lydia J.
Mendel : illustrated by Normand Chartier.
      p.   cm.
  Summary: Spending Christmas in Florida with his grandparents,
David is surprised that there is no snow and that his winter clothes
are too warm for him.
  ISBN 0-395-60196-7
  [1. Florida—Fiction.   2. Christmas—Fiction.   3. Clothing and
dress—Fiction.]   I. Mendel, Lydia.   II. Chartier, Normand, 1945–
ill.   III. Title.
PZ7.J7792A1   1993   91-41248
[E]—dc20   CIP
                            AC

Printed in the United States of America

BP   10   9   8   7   6   5   4   3   2   1

David was excited. He was going to spend Christmas with his grandparents, who lived in Florida. David had visited his grandparents in Florida before, but never for Christmas. As long as David could remember, Christmas had been spent at his home in Maine.

He was leaving tomorrow. As he snuggled up to Mr. Moose, he thought of snowmen and snowballs and snowflakes.

When David woke up the next morning, he saw that his parents had already packed a suitcase for him. But David wanted to pack one, too. His parents gave him a little blue suitcase for the important things he needed to bring.

On the way to the airport, Mr. Moose sat in David's lap, watching the light snow fall on the green pine trees.

They took off as the sun was going down. Mr. Moose had never been on a plane before, so David gave him the window seat.

When the plane landed, David and Mr. Moose were asleep.

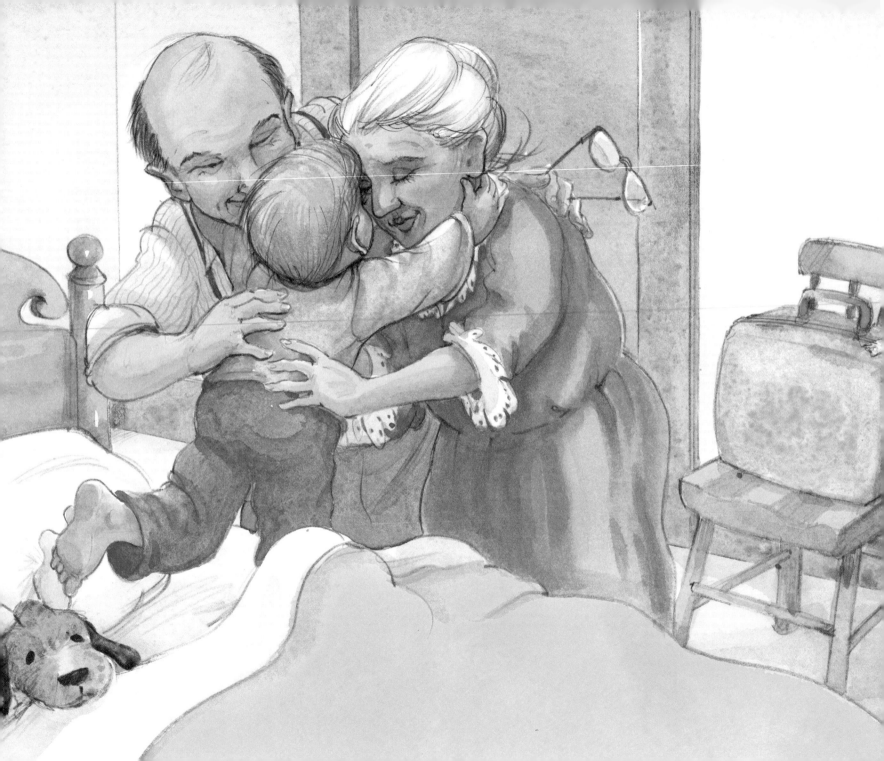

David opened his eyes as his grandparents were tucking him in bed. He said hello and gave them kisses. He asked for a glass of milk. He saw his little blue suitcase sitting on a chair against the wall. That night, David dreamed about snowmen and snowballs and snowflakes.

David woke up very early the next morning. His parents were still sleeping. Grandmother had not yet gotten up. Grandfather was making breakfast when David asked if he could go out and play. David was going to make a Christmas snowman for his grandparents.

Carefully he unzipped his suitcase. He pulled out his long underwear and put it on—*all by himself.*

He put on his thick socks—*all by himself.*

He put on his striped pants—*all by himself.*

He put on his turtleneck—*all by himself.*

Then David put on his scarf and snowsuit—*all by himself.*

Finally, David managed to put on his boots, hat, and mittens—*all by himself.*

David was warm. But he was always warm in his winter clothes until he was out in the snow.

David waddled out of his bedroom and over to the front door. He quietly opened the door and stood there, blinking in the bright sunshine.

He looked around for the snow. He couldn't see any. "Where could it be?" thought David. "Maybe it's by the side of the house." He was feeling warmer.

David took off his hat and mittens and put them on the porch. Then he walked out to the front yard. He unzipped his snowsuit and took a few more steps. He was quite warm by now.

David sat down to pull off his boots so he could remove his snowsuit.
He left them on the grass and continued to the side of the house.

When he got there, he found more green grass and no snow. "It must be in the backyard," he said to Mr. Moose. David had begun to perspire, so he took off his scarf and placed it on the grass.

Then he took a few steps and stopped. He unbuttoned his striped pants and unzipped the zipper. They had to come off. David was too hot!

When he rounded the corner to the back of the house, David saw a surprising sight. Green grass and no snow! He pulled off his turtleneck and stared.

Over in the back corner of the yard was something that caught his eye. He walked over. David set Mr. Moose down for a moment while he pulled off his long underwear.

David's grandmother walked out of her bedroom and saw the front door open. A hat and a pair of mittens were lying on the porch.

In the front yard were a pair of boots and a child's snowsuit. "This is curious," she thought.

Then she found a scarf.

David's grandmother began to smile. There was a pair of striped pants a short distance away.

Next came a turtleneck.

David's grandmother walked across the back yard, picking up the long underwear on the way.

David turned to his grandmother and said, "Merry Christmas, Grandma. I couldn't find any snow." She put his clothes down on top of the thick socks that were next to the sandbox, and she stepped in to give David a big hug and kiss. "Merry Christmas," she said. "This is the most beautiful sandman I've ever seen."